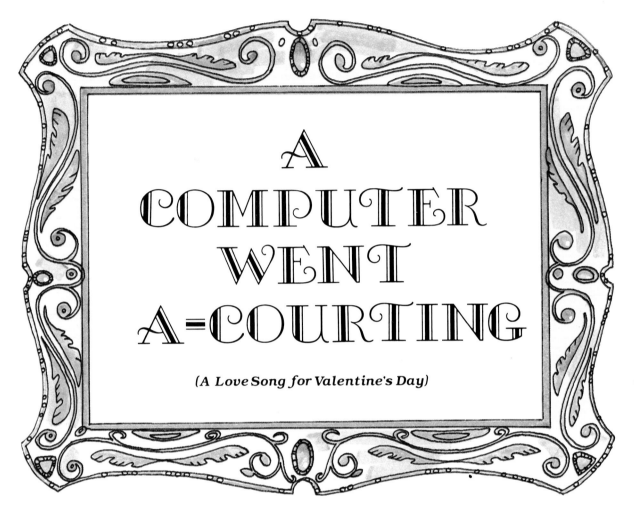

A COMPUTER WENT A-COURTING

(A Love Song for Valentine's Day)

By Carol Greene

Illustrations by Tom Dunnington

CHILDRENS PRESS, CHICAGO

This book is for Andrew

Library of Congress Cataloging in Publication Data

Greene, Carol.
    A computer went a-courting.

    (Sing-along holiday stories)
    Summary: Relates the courtship and marriage of a
computer and robot to the tune of the American folk
song "Frog Went A-courtin'." Includes music.
    1. Children's songs—United States. [1. Computers—
Songs and music.   2.   Robots—Songs and music.
3.   Songs]   I.   Title.
PZ8.3.G82Co   1983   784.6'2405   83-7346
ISBN 0-516-08232-9

A computer went a-courting and he did ride,
Bleep-bleep, Flash-flash.
A computer went a-courting and he did ride,
His disks and printouts by his side,
Bleep-bleep, Bleep-bleep, Flash-flash.

He rode up to Miss Mousie's door,
Bleep-bleep, Flash-flash.
He rode up to Miss Mousie's door,
And kneeled down (which was quite a chore),
Bleep-bleep, Bleep-bleep, Flash-flash.

He put in Program Fourteen-B,
Bleep-bleep, Flash-flash.
He put in Program Fourteen-B,
And said, "Miss Mousie will you marry me?"
Bleep-bleep, Bleep-bleep, Flash-flash.

Miss Mousie said, "Oh, yes—today!"
Bleep-bleep, Flash-flash.
Miss Mousie said, "Oh, yes—today!
But I don't know what my folks will say."
Bleep-bleep, Bleep-bleep, Flash-flash.

So off they went to City Hall,
Bleep-bleep, Flash-flash.
So off they went to City Hall,
And traffic slowed down to a crawl,
Bleep-bleep, Bleep-bleep, Flash-flash.

The computer pushed a button and said, "I do."
Bleep-bleep, Flash-flash.
The computer pushed a button and said, "I do."
And little Miss Mousie squeaked, "Me too."
Bleep-bleep, Bleep-bleep, Flash-flash.

"And where will the wedding supper be?"
Bleep-bleep, Flash-flash.
"And where will the wedding supper be?"
"Oh, anywhere with electricity."
Bleep-bleep, Bleep-bleep, Flash-flash.

"And can you tell me the menu, please?"
Bleep-bleep, Flash-flash.
"And can you tell me the menu, please?"
"A thousand amps and a piece of cheese."
Bleep-bleep, Bleep-bleep, Flash-flash.

Then off they went in a red canoe,
Bleep-bleep, Flash-flash.
Then off they went in a red canoe,
Until the computer's circuits blew,
Bleep-bleep, Bleep-bleep, Flash-flash.

A passing porpoise towed them in,
Bleep-bleep, Flash-flash.
A passing porpoise towed them in.
They said, "We won't do that again."
Bleep-bleep, Bleep-bleep, Flash-flash.

They built a house of brick and wood,
Bleep-bleep, Flash-flash.
They built a house of brick and wood,
And worked in the garden whenever they could,
Bleep-bleep, Bleep-bleep, Flash-flash.

A happy family they became,
Bleep-bleep, Flash-flash.
A happy family they became,
Their first child was a video game,
Bleep-bleep, Bleep-bleep, Flash-flash.

This song is going on the shelf,

Bleep-bleep, Flash-flash.

This song is going on the shelf,

If you want anymore, then sing it yourself,

Bleep-bleep, Bleep-bleep, OVERLOAD!

2. He rode up to Miss Mousie's door,
   Bleep-bleep, Flash-flash.
He rode up to Miss Mousie's door,
   Bleep-bleep, Flash-flash.
He rode up to Miss Mousie's door,
And Kneeled down (which was quite a chore).
   Bleep-bleep, Bleep-bleep, Flash-flash.

3. He put in Program Fourteen B,
   Bleep-bleep, Flash-flash
He put in Program Fourteen
   Bleep-bleep, Flash-flash.
He put in Program Fourteen B,
And said, "Miss Mousie, will you marry me?"
   Bleep-bleep, Bleep-bleep, Flash-flash.

4. Miss Mousie said, "Oh yes, today!"
   Bleep-bleep, Flash-flash.
Miss Mousie said, "Oh yes, today!"
   Bleep-bleep, Flash-flash.
Miss Mousie said "Oh yes, today!
But I don't Know what my folks will say."
   Bleep-bleep, Bleep-bleep, Flash-flash.

5. So off they went to City Hall,
   Bleep-bleep, Flash-flash.
So off they went to City Hall,
   Bleep-bleep, Flash-flash.
So off they went to City Hall,
And traffic slowed down to a crawl,
   Bleep-bleep, Bleep-bleep, Flash-flash.

About the Author

Carol Greene has a B.A. in English Literature from Park College, Parkville, Missouri and an M.A. in Musicology from Indiana University, Bloomington. She's worked with international exchange programs, taught music and writing, and edited children's books. She now works as a free-lance writer in St. Louis, Missouri and has had published over 20 books for children and a few for adults. When she isn't writing, Ms. Greene likes to read, travel, sing, and do volunteer work at her church. Her other books for Childrens Press include: *The Super Snoops and the Missing Sleepers; Sandra Day O'Connor: First Woman on the Supreme Court; Rain! Rain!; Please, Wind?; Snow Joe;* and *The New True Book of Holidays Around the World.*

About the Artist

Tom Dunnington divides his time between book illustration and wildlife painting. He has done many books for Childrens Press, as well as working on textbooks, and is a regular contributor to *Highlights for Children.* Tom lives in Oak Park, Illinois.